To all my little dragons:
Isaac, Paul, Maija, Micah, Levi, and Liam.
— TLG

For Emma, with love.
— EB

How to Dress a
DRAGON

By Thelma Lynne Godin
Pictures by Eric Barclay

Scholastic Press • New York

If you have to dress a dragon, you must be prepared to catch him as he flies by.

You may have to tickle-tackle him to the floor and give him belly kisses.

Once your dragon is still,
it will be time to put on
his underwear.

The good thing is, dragons love underwear.

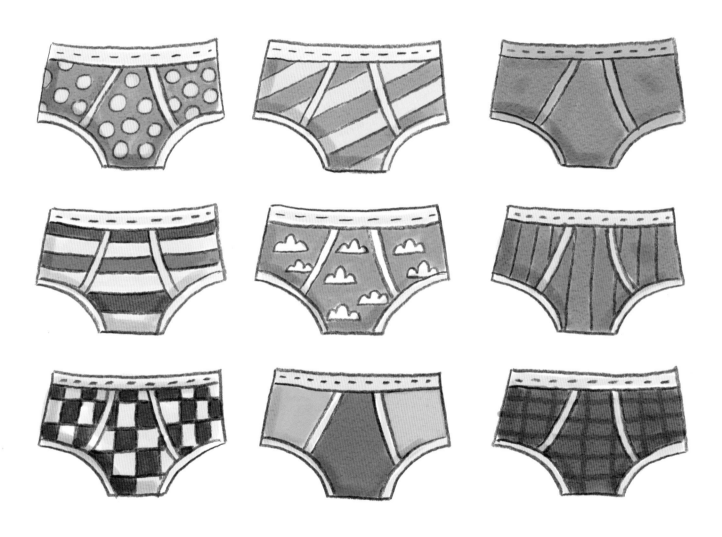

Especially froggy superhero ones.

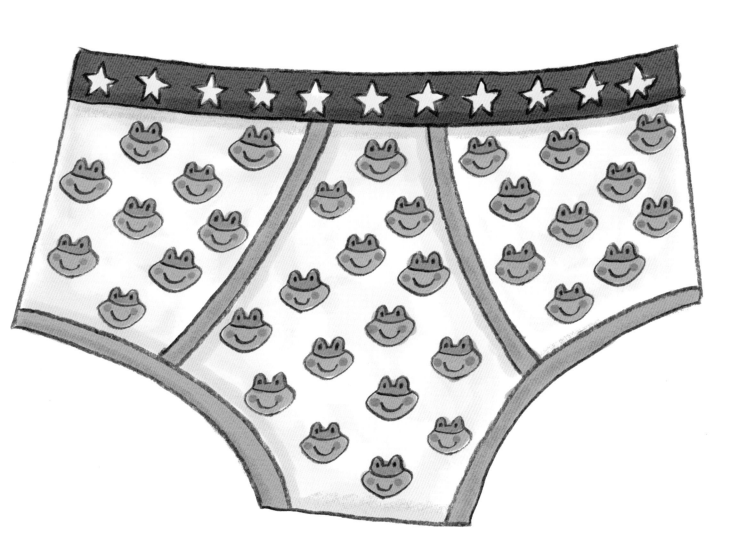

You might have to sit-saddle
your dragon to put on his socks.
Dragons have very ticklish toes.

Dragons do not like
shirts with buttons.

Dragons do not like shirts
that pull over their heads.

DRAGONS...DO...NOT...

But they do like capes.

Dragons prefer shorts instead of pants.

Shorts are much
easier to put on
with big dragon feet.

Shoes can be tricky.

But if you let your dragon wear his froggy boots, he will be very happy.

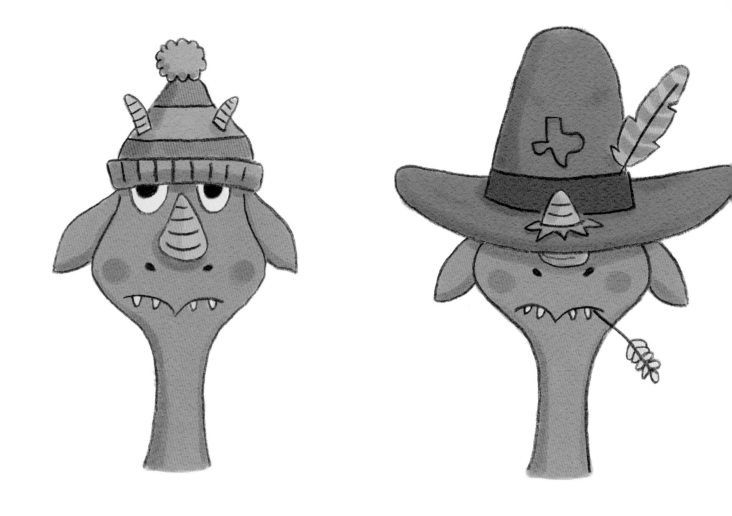

Dragons are very picky about hats.

They will only wear ones that fit
nicely between their horns.

When your dragon is all dressed, he will want to go outside and play.

But beware! If he wants to play his favorite game of Dragon and Knight, your dragon will insist on being the . . .

Library of Congress Cataloging-in-Publication Data
Godin, Thelma Lynne, author.
How to dress a dragon / by Thelma Lynne Godin ; illustrated by Eric Barclay.   pages cm
Summary: A small child helps his reluctant, toddlerlike dragon get dressed.
ISBN 978-0-545-67846-9 (jacketed hardcover)
1. Dragons—Juvenile fiction. 2. Clothing and dress—Juvenile fiction. 3. Imagination—
Juvenile fiction. [1. Dragons—Fiction. 2. Clothing and dress—Fiction. 3. Toddlers—Fiction.]
I. Barclay, Eric, illustrator. II. Title.
PZ7.G54372Ho 2016   [E]—dc23   2014031070

10 9 8 7 6 5 4 3 2 1   16 17 18 19 20

Printed in Malaysia   108
First edition, February 2016

The display type was set in Griffy.
The text was set in Century Schoolbook, and Love Ya Like a Sister.
The illustrations were rendered in pencil on paper and colored digitally.
Book design by Patti Ann Harris and Leslie Mechanic